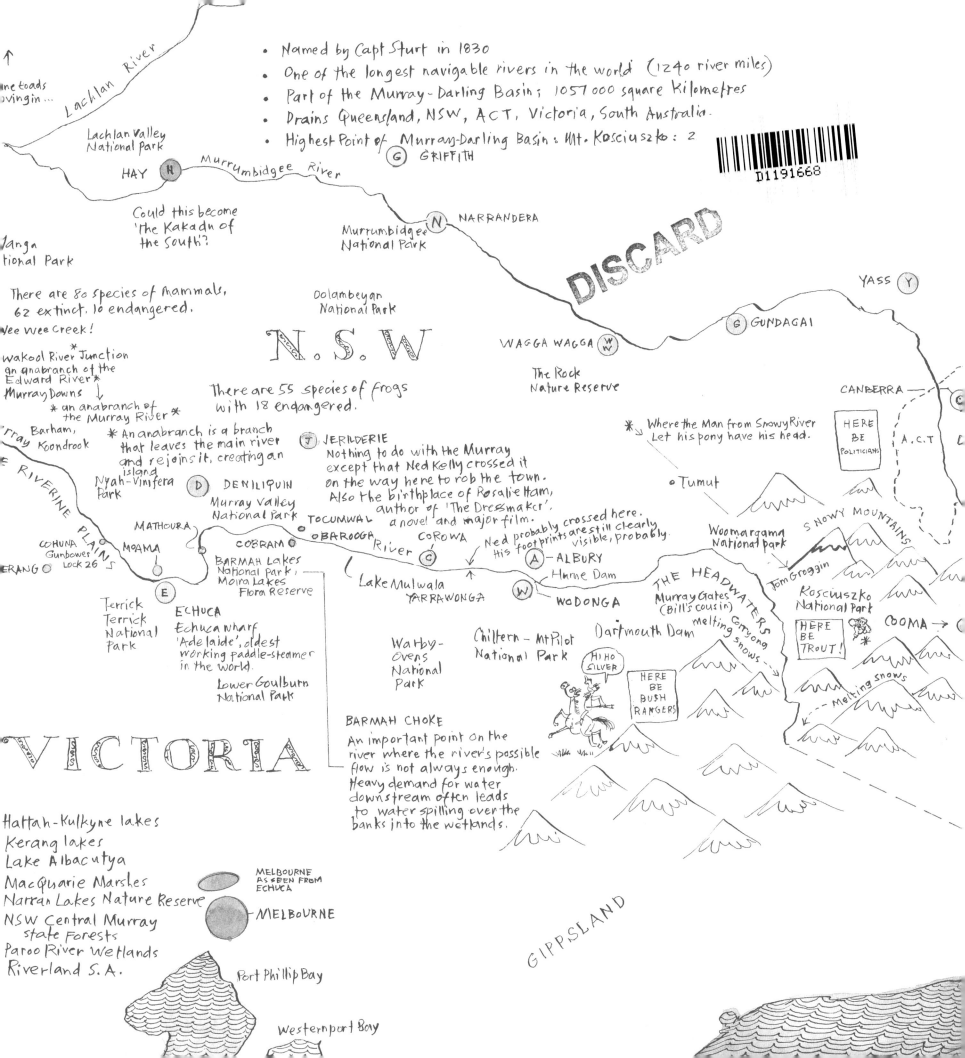

To Nana Grace and Poppa Neil.
Thanks for showing my family the Coorong.
From Anika

When I was younger, I took Roland Harvey
on a trip down the river.
Can you find him on every page?

On the River

Roland Harvey

ALLEN&UNWIN

SYDNEY • MELBOURNE • AUCKLAND • LONDON

Each year, as the winter snow falls on the mountains,
the currawongs head down to the valleys, and the mountains
are silent under their new white blanket.

In spring, as the snows melt and the streams roar,
the currawongs return to feast on the new hatches of bogong moths.
The mountains explode in a riot of flowers.

Here in the foothills, tadpoles practise to be grown-up frogs
in crystal-clear ponds, surrounded by wiry grasses
and tough little plants that have spent the winter sleeping under the snow.
Small fish dart to and fro, hidden beneath overhanging grasses,
and brightly coloured beetles go exploring in the green moss beds.

These are the headwaters of the Murray River,
where this story begins.

The bogong moth migrates to spend the summer in the Australian Alps.

toothbrush
passport
clean undies
sunblock
towel
socks
rod + reel
bait

At Cowombat Flat, mossy bogs and little rivulets link arms.
Here you can stand in two states at once, watching a game of interstate cricket.
This is the border between New South Wales and Victoria.

MOUTH 2508 km

A long time ago, at Tom Groggin, Banjo Paterson was visiting a stockman called Jack Riley. The story Jack told him that day inspired Banjo's poem 'The Man from Snowy River'.

Less well known is the story of Jack Riley's mum's mum, the Gran from Snowy River, who never became as famous as her grandson but was also a very good horse rider.

And after you've caught five or six big trout, and have recited 'The Man from Snowy River' a couple of dozen times, you can go eight kilometres downstream to the serious white water of the Murray Gates.

The descent down the narrow gorge called Murray Gates turns out to be a lot quicker than walking. These rapids are for serious thrill-seekers only.

Correct position

incorrect

O.K.

PARTS OF A CANOE

back

front

emergency
equipment

Book of
Prayers

stretcher

Signalling
devices

Lake Hume is forty metres deep and holds three million megalitres of water — that's six times as much as Sydney Harbour. There are lots of things to do on the lakes. Don't waste a moment looking for bunyips, though — there aren't any, and it would be so much more fun to read about flood mitigation and hydropower, water supply and irrigation.

SKI ETIQUETTE

Good!

Not good.

Worse.

In the Murray River Wetlands you might see:

an Australasian grebe

superb parrot

Australasian bittern;
southern turnip

once bittern

superb local

a canoe tree

Occasionally the river floods and revives the huge ancient river red gums.

You might catch:

a Murray cod
(put him back!)

a carp
(don't put him back!)

a freshwater catfish
(purrfect!)

a cold

Early morning at Echuca Wharf is a quiet and peaceful time. You can have a cup of tea aboard the oldest working paddle-steamer in the world, the *P.S. Adelaide.*

side view

kitchen; toilet

towing post

captain

stem post

funnel

boiler

Front

rudder

stern

waterline

river bed

paddlewheel

Echuca is also home to the paddle-steamers *Etona*, *Pride of the Murray*, *Canberra*, *Alexander Arbuthnot*, *Emmylou*, *Pevensey* and *Hero*. This is the largest collection of working paddle-steamers in the world.

BUMBOATS
were small hand-driven side wheelers, used by fishermen, shearers, hawkers, tinkers, travelling photographers and anyone else with a bum.

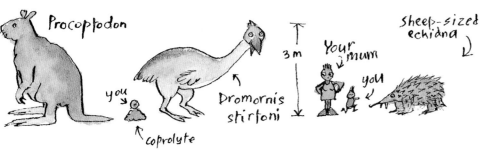

Procoptodon

you

↑ coprolyte

Dromornis stirtoni

3 m

Your mum

you

Sheep-sized echidna

40 000 years ago, Aboriginal people lived at Lake Mungo, hunting giant kangaroos and giant wombats, eating emu eggs and shellfish. 150 years ago, young Canadian brothers George and W.B. Chaffey moved to nearby Mildura and introduced irrigation.

After World War I, soldier settlers joined the locals in Mildura, along with immigrants from Italy, Ireland, Greece, England and Yugoslavia, each contributing to the rich and diverse city it is today. The food is good as well.

Normal Easiest Intermediate Hard Advanced

Hello Darling,

I'm sorry to hear you've been in poor health. Of course it's easy to say, but high salt content and chronic drought would make any river sick. Better management and increased rainfall should greatly increase your flow, and I would strongly recommend you act to reduce the number of discharges you are experiencing. Furthermore,

might I prescribe a complete break from pesticides. Unfortunately unless you can undertake these steps, one can do little to help and you may remain embarrassingly small and rather shallow.

Yours sincerely,
Murray

Lake Victoria is a natural lake adapted to act as a reservoir, to compensate for droughts as far up as Queensland and keep the Murray flowing.

Locks help boats to travel up and downstream.

G.O.   Gate open
G.S.   Gate shut
V.O.   Valve open

G.O.   G.S.   G.S.   G.S. V.O   G.S.   G.O.

The labyrinthine river threads through a mosaic of fruit blocks, flood plains, anabranches and billabongs. These wetlands are important habitat for birds and wildlife.

The trees and wildlife need regular small floods for seeding, breeding and feeding. These floods sometimes don't happen enough, as the river's water is diverted to feed crops.

The river works hard to feed both us —
our farms and our drinking-water dams —
and the natural landscape.

Along the famous red cliffs, where oranges, peaches and wine grapes grow, you will find fossilised seashells embedded in the golden ochre sandstone. They are 20 million years old.

The 'Wine Beard'

Early attempts were an udder failure

Hand

1911

'wine cushions' were popular until chilled wine became fashionable

An interesting idea by New Zealanders Nick and Bec Payne was abandoned for medical reasons

1940 good!

1965 better!

* CAUTION! Can lead to a condition called 'Cask finger'

Thomas William Carlyon Angove invented the 'wine in a box' idea in 1965.

Mannum is a very old town, still
largely in black-and-white.

Here in 1852...
❑ Captain William Randell
❑ Sir Thomas Paddle Steamer
   (tick correct box)
built the first paddle steamer in Australia.

CAUTION
THIS NOTICE IS
SO LONG AND
WORDY YOU
WON'T HAVE
TIME TO READ IT
AS YOU RUSH
FAST INTO A
NEW TIME ZONE

He had no plans and had never seen a
paddle steamer. It worked well, except
the first boiler nearly blew them all up.

Can you spot the small inaccuracy
in this picture?

Goolwa Barrage was one of five barrages built to try to keep the river's fresh water separate from the salty sea above the river's mouth. This means farmers upstream can use the fresh water for their crops.

The nearby Coorong — where seawater, river water, rainwater and groundwater all naturally meet — was once one of Australia's most important sites for birds. But their numbers fell drastically when the river's mouth closed and the water became toxic.

Lots of action is being taken to help keep the river healthy and to balance the needs of industry — communities and farmers, fruit-growers and winemakers — with the needs of people and nature.

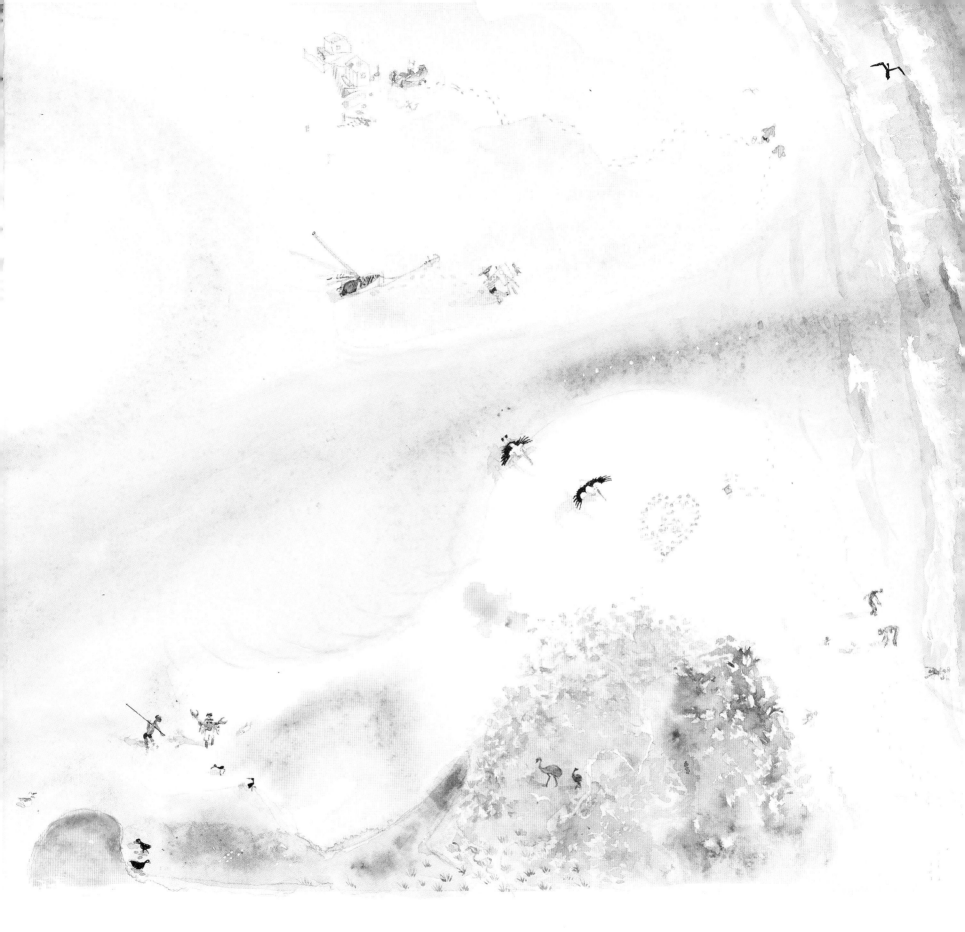

Recently some children made a heart shape on the sand at the Murray mouth to show their love for the river. That's surely a good sign.

As our story ends, the river's mouth
is open again and the Murray's water is flowing to the sea.
Salt and fresh water mix again, and the fish and birds are returning.
The river is coming back to life.

Thanks to the teachers and children at Mannum Primary School,
and all the other wonderful people I met in my travels along the Murray.
R.H.

First published by Allen & Unwin in 2016

Allen & Unwin – Australia
83 Alexander Street, Crows Nest NSW 2065, Australia
Phone: (61 2) 8425 0100
Email: info@allenandunwin.com
Web: www.allenandunwin.com

Allen & Unwin – UK
Ormond House, 26–27 Boswell Street,
London WC1N 3JZ, UK
Phone: +44 (0) 20 8785 5995
Email: info@murdochbooks.co.uk
Web: www.murdochbooks.co.uk

A Cataloguing-in-Publication entry is available
from the National Library of Australia
www.trove.nla.gov.au.
A catalogue record for this book is available from the British Library.

ISBN (AUS) 978 1 76011 245 5
ISBN (UK) 978 1 74336 866 4

Teachers' notes available from www.allenandunwin.com

Cover and text design by Sandra Nobes
Set in Harvey, created by Sandra Nobes from Roland Harvey's handwriting
Colour reproduction by Splitting Image, Clayton, Victoria
This book was printed in March 2016 at Hang Tai Printing (Guang Dong) Ltd, China.

1 3 5 7 9 10 8 6 4 2

www.rolandharvey.com.au

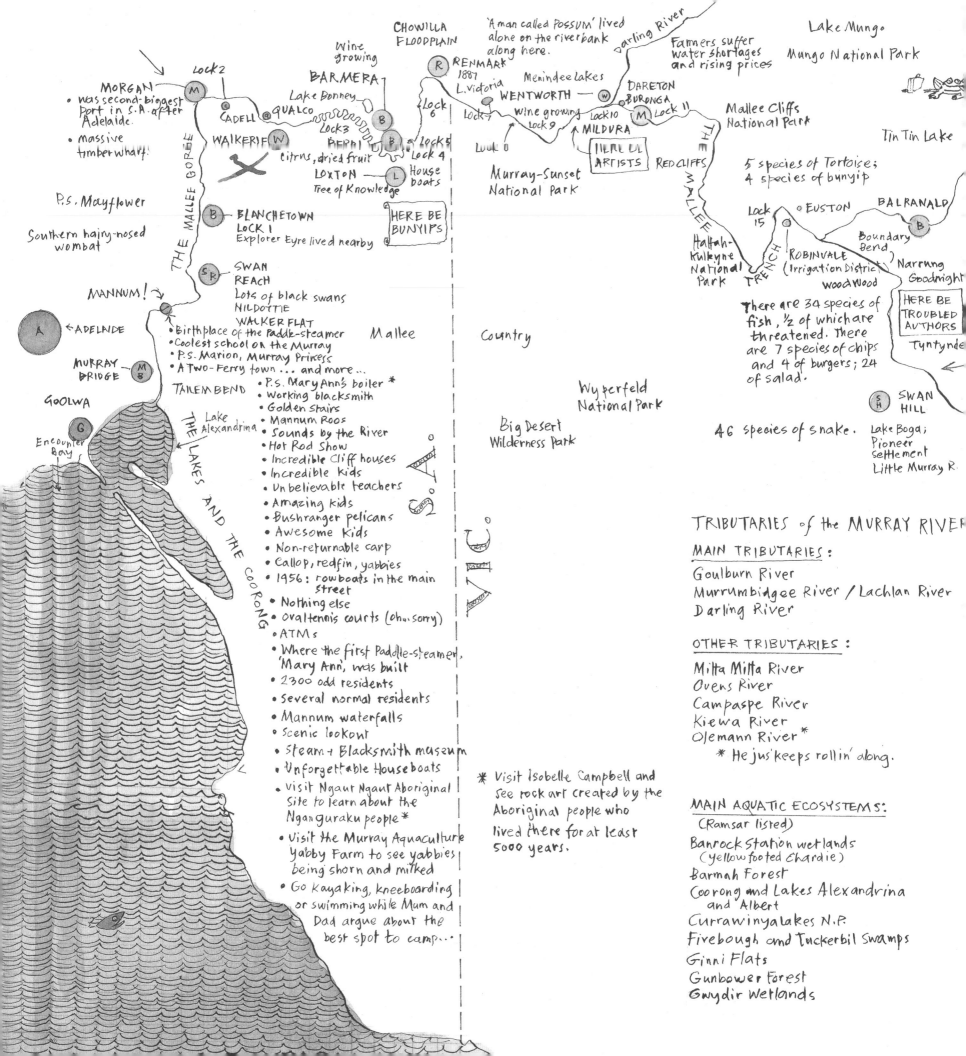